Mel Bay's

SONGS of CHRISTMAS for AUTOHARP®

BY MEG PETERSON AND DAN FOX

1 2 3 4 5 6 7 8 9 0

PREFACE

Here is a collection of Christmas songs and carols from many lands, arranged especially for the Autoharp® and Chromaharp®.

We assume that the player has mastered simple strumming techniques on the instrument and knows the fundamentals of Autoharp playing, pressing the chord bar button firmly with one hand while stroking the strings with the other.

We have gone beyond the usual simple chording in most of the arrangements, since the true beauty of many of these classic carols lies in the richness of the many harmonic changes. The basic chord arrangement is shown above the words, followed by slashes (/) which mean to stroke the same chord until a new one appears.

The chords in small italics under the music are for melody playing. By changing chords more frequently the melody will emerge.° This may be done by stroking upwards as far as the melody note or by pinching gently with the thumb or index finger in the area of the melody note. This is not difficult since several strings on either side of the melody string (or note) are blanked out by the chord bar. Experiment, using simple short strokes as first, until you hear the melody. You can use a thumb and finger pick for more accuracy.

Each slash (/) in melody playing represents a specific melody note to be pinched or stroked, and the small arrows (∕) denote gentle brushes in the lower octave with the thumb to keep the rhythm going.

Sometimes the chords used for melody playing are different from those appearing in the basic arrangement above the words. This has been done to facilitate playing when fast changes occur, as well as to give the player a variety of harmonizations.

Most songs in this book are arranged for the 15 chord instrument. However, some songs require chords not found on that particular model. This is noted under the title by the words: 21 or 27 chord model.

If a chord is in parentheses it can be substituted for the preferred chord which appears in the arrangement.

The musical term D.C. is an abbreviation for Da Capo, meaning "from the beginning."

Fine (pronounced fee-nay) means "the end."

Therefore, the phrase D.C. al Fine means to go back to the beginning of the piece and play to the end, stopping at the word "Fine."

Amplifying the Autoharp or Chromaharp and playing it in a variety of styles from simple strumming to melody picking is an exciting way to enhance these beautiful old traditional songs and carols. Many players use a soft felt pick which gives the amplified instrument an organ-like quality especially adapted to a church or concert hall.

I hope this book will add joy and musical cheer to your holiday season!

Meg Peterson

°*For study of melody picking see: The Complete Method For Autoharp Or Chromaharp, Meg Peterson, Mel Bay Publications, 1979.*

CONTENTS

Angels We Have Heard on High

Moderately   **Traditional**

Break Forth O Beauteous Heav'nly Light
(21 or 27 Chord Model)

Words by Johann Rist

Firmly

Music by
Johann Schop

Bring a Torch Jeannette Isabella

The Cherry Tree Carol

Traditional

Slowly

When Jo - seph was an old___ man, An old man was___

he, He___ mar - ried Vir - gin Mar - y, The___

Queen of Ga - li - lee, He ___ mar - ried Vir - gin

Mar - y, The___ Queen of Ga - li - lee.

The Coventry Carol
(21 Chord Model)

Gently, like a lullaby

Traditional

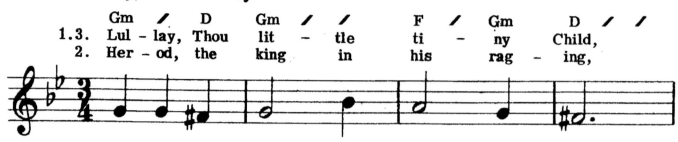

1.3. Lul – lay, Thou lit – tle ti – ny Child,
2. Her – od, the king in his rag – ing,

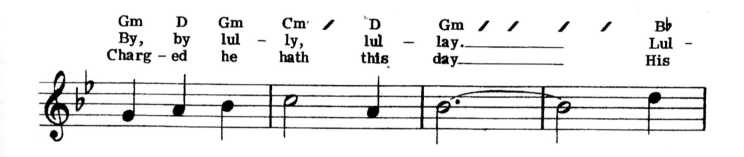

By, by lul – ly, lul – lay._____ Lul –
Charg – ed he hath this day_____ His

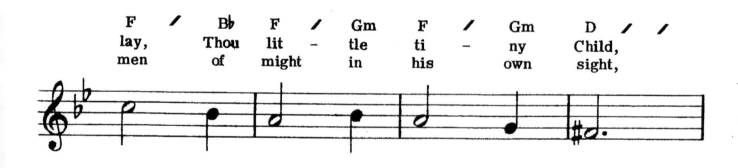

lay, Thou lit – tle ti – ny Child,
men of might in his own sight,

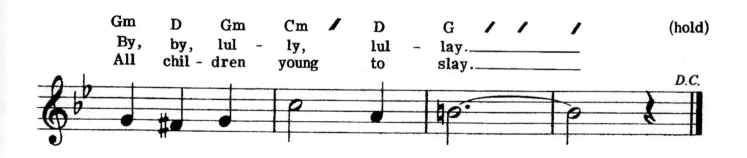

By, by, lul – ly, lul – lay._____
All chil – dren young to slay._____

(hold)

D.C.

Deck the Halls

Traditional

With spirit

The First Noel

Moderately

Traditional

Go Tell It on the Mountain

Traditional

God Rest Ye, Merry Gentlemen

Brightly

Traditional

Good Christian Men, Rejoice

Moderately   German

Good King Wenceslas

Words by
John Neale

Music
Traditional

Hark the Herald Angels Sing

Word by
Charles Wesley

Music by
Felix Mendelssohn

1. Hark! the her-ald an-gels sing, — Glo-ry to the new-born King;
2. Hail the heav'n-born Prince of Peace Hail the Sun of Right-eous-ness!

Peace on earth and mer-cy mild,____God and sin-ners re-con-ciled.
Light of life to all He brings,____Ris'n with heal-ing in his wings.

Joy-ful, all ye na-tions rise,__ Join the tri-umph of the skies;__
Mild he lays His glo-ry by,__ Born that no more men would die__

With th'an-gel-ic host pro-claim, "Christ is__born in Beth-le-hem!"
Born to raise the song of earth, Born to__give them sec-ond birth.

Hark! the her-ald an-gels sing, "Glo-ry__to the new born King."

I Saw Three Ships

Away in a Manger

It Came Upon the Midnight Clear

Words by
Edmund Sears

Music by
Richard Willis

Jingle Bells

Words and Music
by J. Pierpont

Jolly Old St. Nicholas

Traditional

Joy to the World

Words by
Isaac Watts

Music by
Lowell Mason

1. Joy to the world the Lord is come; Let
2. Joy to the earth the Sav - ior reigns; Let

earth re - ceive her King; Let ev - 'ry
men their songs em - ploy; While fields and

heart_____ pre - pare_____ Him_____ room,_____ and
floods,_____ rocks, hills_____ and_____ plains,_____ Re -

heav'n and na - ture sing, And___heav'n and na - ture sing, And___
peat the sound-ing joy, Re - peat the sound-ing joy, Re -

heav'n and heav'n___ and na - ture sing.
peat,___ re - peat____ the sound - ing joy.

D.C.

Lo, How a Rose E'er Blooming

Traditional

O Christmas Tree
(Based on 'Oh Tannenbaum')

Traditional

O Come, All Ye Faithful
(Adeste Fideles)

Traditional

1. O Come, all ye faith-ful, Joy-ful and tri-umph-ant, O
2. Sing choirs of an-gels, Sing in ex-ul-ta-tion, O

come ye, O come ye to Beth-le-hem;
Sing all ye cit-i-zens of heav'n a-bove.

Come and be-hold Him, Born the King of An-gels; O
Glo-ry to God In the high-est glo-ry! O

come let us a-dore Him, O come, let us a-dore Him, O

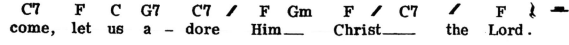

come, let us a-dore Him Christ the Lord.

O Holy Night
(Cantique de Noel)

Words by
J.S. Dwight

Music by
A. Adam

1. O ho - ly night, the stars are bright-ly shin - ing, It is the
2. Led by the light of faith se-rene - ly beam - ing, With glow-ing

night of the dear Sav-ior's birth; Long lay the world in sin and sor - row
heart by His cra-dle we stand; So led by light of a star sweet-ly

pin - ing till He ap-peared and the soul felt its worth. A
gleam-ing, Here came the Wise Men from the Ori-ent land. The

thrill of hope the wea-ry world re-joic - es, For yon-der breaks a
King of kings lay thus in low - ly man-ger. In all our tri - als

new and glo-rious morn! Fall on your knees! O hear the an-gel
born to be our Friend; He knows our need, He guard — eth us from

voi - ces, O night di - vine! O night when Christ was
dan - ger, Be-hold your king! be fore the Low - ly

born! O night di - vine! O night, O night di - vine!
bend! Be-hold your King! be-fore the Low-ly bend!

O Little Town of Bethlehem

Words by
Phillips Brooks

Music by
Lewis Redner

1. O lit – tle town of Beth – le – hem, How still we ___ see thee lie: A – bove thy deep and dream–less sleep The si – lent stars go by; Yet in thy dark streets shin – eth The ev – er – last – ing Light; The hopes and fears of all the years Are met in thee to – night

2. For Christ is born of Mar – ry, And gath–ered all a – bove. While mor – tals sleep, the an – gels keep Their watch of ___ won –d'ring love. O mourn–ing stars, to – geth – er Pro – claim the ho – ly birth: And prais – es sing to God the King, And peace to men on earth.

The Holly and the Ivy

Traditional

Moderately

Silent Night

**Words by
Joseph Mohr**

**Music by
Franz X. Gruber**

Flowing

1. Si - lent night, ho - ly night; All is
2. Si - lent night, ho - ly night; Shep - herds

calm, all is bright Round yon Vir - gin
quake at the bright sight, Glo - ries stream from

Moth - er and Child. Ho - ly In - fant so
heav - en a - far, Heav - 'nly hosts sing

ten - der and mild, Sleep in heav - en - ly
al - le - lu - ia; Christ the Sav - ior is

peace, Sleep in heav - en-ly peace.
born: Christ the Sav - ior is born.

The Twelve Days of Christmas

Moderately

Traditional

We Three Kings

Words and Music by
John H. Hopkins

We Wish You a Merry Christmas

Traditional

What Child is This?
(Based on "Greensleeves")

Gently

Traditional English Carol